The Baby That ROARED

Simon Puttock

illustrated by

Nadia Shireen

For my family
S. P.

Inspired by the energy, wit, and sartorial
stylings of Dr. Haris Ahmed
N. S.

Text copyright © 2012 by Simon Puttock
Illustrations copyright © 2012 by Nadia Shireen

All rights reserved No part of this book may be
reproduced, transmitted, or stored in an information
retrieval system in any form or by any means, graphic,
electronic, or mechanical, including photocopying, taping,
and recording without prior written permission from the
publisher.

First U.S. edition 2012

Library of Congress Catalog Card Number pending

Library of Congress Cataloging-in-Publication Data
is available.

ISBN 978-0-7636-5903-5

11 12 13 14 15 16 HH OH 10 9 8 7 6 5 4 3 2 1

Printed in Heshan, Guangdong, China

This book was typeset in Archetype Regular.
The illustrations were done in mixed media.

Nosy Crow
an imprint of
Candlewick Press
99 Dover Street
Somerville, Massachusetts 02144

www.nosycrow.com
www.candlewick.com

nosy crow

An imprint of Candlewick Press

Mr. and Mrs. Deer had no baby
of their own to love and cuddle
and read stories to. . . .

But, oh!—

how they wished that they did!

ROAR!

Then one day,

they found a bundle on the doorstep.

The bundle had a note attached,

which said:

I am a dear little baby. Please love me and cuddle me and read me lots and Lots of stories.

Mrs. Deer picked it up and cuddled it at once.

Then she popped it into the laundry basket, which was just the right size
for a bed. But no sooner had she put the baby down
than it let out a great big

ROAR!

"I think it's hungry," said Mr. Deer. "Babies usually are."

But the baby didn't want
cheese,

and the baby didn't want
toast,

and the baby
didn't want
cabbage,

or **cucumbers,**

or **cauliflower!**

What **did** the baby **want** to eat?

"We must get Uncle Duncan," said Mrs. Deer. "He's bound to know."

A baby?
A dear little baby?
I shall come at once.

"Babies
need milk,"
said Uncle Duncan.
"You must warm some
up immediately."

But . . .

when Mr. and Mrs. Deer came back—how very peculiar!
Uncle Duncan had disappeared, and the baby was still

ROARING!

"Ew!" said Mr. Deer. "I think this baby needs
changing. We must ask Auntie Agnes—
she generally knows what's what."

A baby?
A dear little baby?

I shall come at once!

"**Diapers!**" said Auntie Agnes.
"And clean towels and special
ointment, too!
Now, run along and fetch them,
quick as you can."

But . . .

when Mr. and Mrs. Deer came
back—how very peculiar!
Auntie Agnes had disappeared,
and the baby was still roaring!

"Oh, poor little baby,"
said Mr. Deer.
"Whatever shall we do?"

"Perhaps," said Mrs. Deer, "it isn't feeling very well. We must call Dr. Fox to come and take a look."

ROAR!

A baby?
A dear little baby?
I shall come at once!

"I shall need **peace** and **quiet** to examine the baby," said Dr. Fox.

"Now, run along, you two,
and leave everything to me."

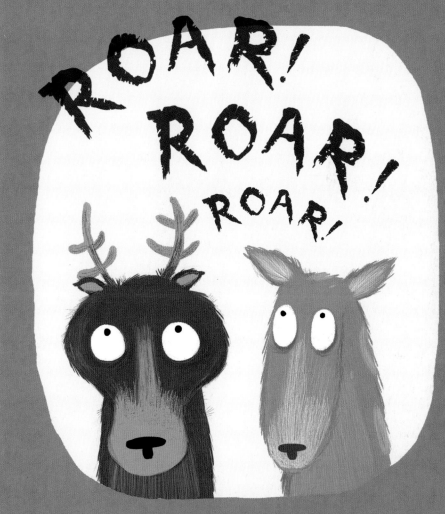

Mr. and Mrs. Deer ran along,
and waited, and waited,
and waited.

ROAR!
ROAR!
ROAR!

But the baby went on roaring.
They had to know
what was happening,
so they tiptoed in and . . .

How very **peculiar**!
Dr. **Fox** had disappeared
and the baby was still

ROARING!

"Oh, no," said Mrs. Deer.
"What shall we do now?"

"Granny Bear,"
said Mr. Deer,
"will know exactly
what to do."

Granny Bear came at once.
She took one look at the poor little,
dear little, roaring, **roaring**
baby and said,

"I know **exactly** what to do.
This baby needs **burping**."

And she picked up the
baby and patted it,

and  it,

and **patted** it,

until . . .

It was really very **peculiar!**

Out came
Uncle Duncan,

and out came
Auntie Agnes,

and out came

Dr. Fox, too!

And none of them looked the

least bit pleased.

"That's not a dear little baby!"
cried Granny Bear.
"That is a LITTLE MON